Fortress

A One-Act Play

by
Michael Scanlan

Baker's Plays
7611 Sunset Blvd.
Los Angeles, CA 90046
bakersplays.com

NOTICE

This book is offered for sale at the price quoted only on the understanding that, if any additional copies of the whole or any part are necessary for its production, such additional copies will be purchased. The attention of all purchasers is directed to the following: This work is protected under the copyright laws of the United States of America, in the British Empire, including the Dominion of Canada, and all other countries adhering to the Universal Copyright Convention. Violations of the Copyright Law are punishable by fine or imprisonment, or both. The copying or duplication of this work or any part of this work, by hand or by any process, is an infringement of the copyright and will be vigorously prosecuted.

This play may not be produced by amateurs or professionals for public or private performance without first submitting application for performing rights. Licensing fees are due on all performances whether for charity or gain, or whether admission is charged or not Since performance of this play without the payment of the licensing fee renders anybody participating liable to severe penalties imposed by the law, anybody acting in this play should be sure, before doing so, that the royalty fee has been paid. Professional rights, reading rights, radio broadcasting, television and all mechanical rights, etc. are strictly reserved. Application for performing rights should be made directly to BAKER'S PLAYS.

No one shall commit or authorize any act or omission by which the copyright of, or the right to copyright, this play may be impaired. No one shall make any changes in this play for the purpose of production.

Publication of this play does not imply availability for performance. Both amateurs and professionals considering a production are strongly advised in their own interest to apply to Baker's Plays for written permission before starting rehearsals, advertising, or booking a theatre.

Whenever the play is produced, the author's name must be carried in all publicity, advertising and programs. Also, the following notice must appear on all printed programs, "Produced by special arrangement with Baker's Plays."

Licensing fees for FORTRESS is based on a per performance rate and payable one week in advance of the production.
Please consult the Baker's Plays website at www.bakersplays.com or our current print catalogue for up to date licensing fee information.

FORTRESS
978-0-87440-882-9
179-B

FORTRESS was developed during 1986-1987 with students from LaSalle Academy in Providence, Rhode Island.

First preformed in earlier versions during the spring and fall of 1986 at LaSalle Academy, Providence, Rhode Island with the following cast:

KIM — *Karen Chapasko*

BILLY — *Steve Gomes* (Spring), *Erich Gottshalk* (Fall)

ENSEMBLE — *Billy Angell, Chris Caldarone, Robert Casey, Courtney Daragan, Stefanie Di.Maio, Diane Gilcreast, Suzanne Johnson, Michael Karkos, Mary Ann Maiorisi, Dean McClain, Amanda McKnight, John O'Connell, Christen O'Haire, Robert Sieczkiewicz*

PRODUCTION STAGE MGR. — *Kevin Smith*

First performed in a revised version on July 10, 1987 at the Project Discovery Playwright's Workshop, Choate Rosemary Hall, Wallingford, Conn. under the direction of Joanna Blake and Ron Emmons with the following cast:

BILLY — *Joe Mazza*

KIM — *Emily Lazar*

ENSEMBLE — *Valerie Aaronoff, Kari Braeger, Kim Brooks, Christopher Clark, Portia Dawson, Justin Goodyear, Sara Hand, Dara Herman, Karin Hoppenbouwers, Bengt Jonsson, Anne Longsworth, Christopher Moss, Skie Ocasio, Edmund Redfield, Drew Seider, Eric Seid*

ASST. TO THE DIRECTORS — *Andrew Glasfeld*

THE CAST

Billy, a High School Senior
Kim, a High School Senior
The Ensemble assumes all other roles

STAGING

FORTRESS lends itself to flexible staging techniques.

— The only set pieces which are essential include a number of sturdy wooden chairs.

— For the most part, props should be mimed with the exception of the "Superman" pieces: comic books, Kryptonite, etc.

— Generally, costume changes are to be discouraged. Billy and Kim should wear comfortable clothing appropriate for seniors in high school. Costume pieces such as jackets, the bathrobe and, of course, Billy's Superman paraphernalia can be added. The members of the Ensemble should wear costumes which indicate particular roles: i.e., a suitcoat and a tie for the actor playing Herb, a skirt for Gladys, jeans for the "Kids", etc.

— Lighting can greatly enhance the performances of this play, providing quick changes of scene by use of crossfades and establishing mood.

4

— The Ensemble is an integral part of the action and should remain on stage throughout the play. It can be composed of as few as six members. However, a large Ensemble can be quite effective. The script indicates a number of ways to involve the Ensemble in the action, but imaginative casts and directors will create more opportunities for integration. If a small Ensemble is used, all members should assume the role of Dr. Angle. Feel free to experiment.

TIME

The present and the past

**FORTRESS is also available
as a full length play.**

FORTRESS

A cocktail party at the funeral home. The lights reveal wooden chairs arranged in a wide semicircle, facing center. Members of the ENSEMBLE are "frozen" in "party" poses. After a beat, one of them speaks the opening line and continues to repeat it as each member joins to create a rising wall of party noise.

ENSEMBLE. Party chatter, party chatter, chatter chatter, party chatter. *(When the noise has reached a fevered pitch, it abruptly stops. The ENSEMBLE freezes. KIM enters and speaks to the audience)*

KIM. Love stinks. It's like being trapped in a phone booth with sixteen flatulent people who just came from an all-you-can-eat bean dinner. You think it's funny? Well, it's not. It's depressing. I wish I never laid eyes on Billy Thompson. He's a total gross-out: stupid, selfish, insensitive and about as much fun as an abscessed tooth. All right, so maybe it's not all his fault, maybe his life hasn't been that great. His parents are total waste products. His father, Herb, runs a funeral home. Big deal, huh? A job's a job. But the problem with Herb Thompson is that he *acts* like someone who runs a funeral home — all slick and solemn and stiff. He's the kind of guy who likes working around dead people because they can't talk back. And Billy's mother, Gladys? The biggest trauma in her life was getting too old to be in the Junior League. But the worst thing about the Thompsons, the thing that Billy can never forgive, is that they lied to him. Supposedly because they loved him, because they wanted to protect him. But it all came out one night at one of Gladys' fancy cocktail parties at the funeral home. *(KIM withdraws to watch the scene as the party springs into life)*

ENSEMBLE. *(Moving in a styled manner)* Party chatter, party chatter, chatter chatter, party chatter. *(Fragments of conversation interrupt the general hubbub)* "Believe me, buy on margin and you'll live to regret it..." Chatter, chatter, chatter, chatter. "Miss being married? You have got to be kidding! My dear, you just have no idea what it's like out there..." Chatter chatter. *(Pause)* Chatter chatter. "Do you think someone should tell her how ugly that dress is..." Party chatter, party. "She says he was fixing her furnace..." Ha, ha party chatter. Ha, ha party chatter. "The scar goes from here to... Well, never mind..." Awfully good to party chatter. "They're ruining the country. They are ruining the country..." Chit chat party chatter. Chit chat party chatter. "They just laid down and died. Two innings to go and they just laid down and died..." Party party party party party party party party. "This is good. Isn't this good? Do you think she makes her own mayonnaise..." Party. *(Pause)* Party. "It's the best! All you eat is spinach and beans. Three pounds I lost. Of course, you spend a lot of time in the potty..." *(The party chatter builds until GLADYS spots BILLY offstage)* Party chatter, party chatter, chatter chatter, party chatter.

GLADYS. Billy! Come on in and say goodnight to everyone. Billy! Come on, honey, don't be shy. Oh, Billy...

HERB. *(Aggravated that BILLY still has not entered)* Billy!

GLADYS. Now, Herb, don't be so gruff, for heaven's sake he's only five. *(BILLY enters, dressed in a bathrobe, carrying a teddy bear)*

ENSEMBLE. Aw, isn't he cute!

GLADYS. Billy, give Aunt Margaret a kiss.

AUNT MARGARET. Isn't he just the cutest? *(She kisses him sloppily)* Billy, this is my...friend, Mr. Lawless.

BILLY. *(Extending his hand)* How do you do, sir?

MR. LAWLESS. *(Shaking hands)* Why, I'm fine, thank you. What beautiful manners you have, boy. *(GLADYS beams)*

BILLY. Thank you, sir.

MR. LAWLESS. And so tall. What a big boy you are.

BILLY. Thank you, sir.

MR. LAWLESS. You must knock them dead on the basketball court, eh?

BILLY. No, sir.

MR. LAWLESS. No?

BILLY. No, sir, I don't knock them dead on the basketball court, sir.

MR. LAWLESS. Oh?

BILLY. My mother doesn't like me to play basketball, sir.

MR. LAWLESS. Why is that, boy?

BILLY. *(With GLADYS mouthing the words behind him)* Because when you play basketball, you sweat. And when you sweat you can catch a chill. And when you catch a chill, it can lead to... *(Struggling for the word, and then, proudly...)* AMONIA. You can die from amonia, sir.

MR. LAWLESS. *(Somewhat at a loss for words)* Well...

AUNT MARGARET. *(Trying to save the situation)* Oh, Billy, you are too precious.

BILLY. Thank you, Aunt Margaret.

GLADYS. Come along, Billy. Let's go say goodnight to Uncle Leo.

AUNT MARGARET. Goodnight, sweetie.

BILLY. Goodnight, Aunt Margaret; goodnight, sir. *(BILLY crosses to Up Center and stops with his back to the audience. The ENSEMBLE resumes speaking, at first very softly, but gradually building in volume)*

ENSEMBLE. Party chatter, party chatter, chatter chatter, party chatter.

MR. LAWLESS. *(Speaking over the chatter)* Well, he certainly is...

AUNT MARGARET. ...isn't he?

MR. LAWLESS. And so...

AUNT MARGARET. ...tall?

MR. LAWLESS. Yes. He doesn't look at all like h...

AUNT MARGARET. ...his parents.

MR. LAWLESS. Yes.

AUNT MARGARET. He's not.

MR. LAWLESS. Not?

AUNT MARGARET. *(Over the party noise which has grown quite loud)* Theirs. He's not theirs.

MR. LAWLESS. *(Straining to hear)* What?

AUNT MARGARET. *(The party noise halts abruptly as she shouts)* He's adopted! *(A gasp from the Ensemble)*

MR. LAWLESS. Ah.

AUNT MARGARET. But of course, he doesn't know. *(BILLY turns and looks to Gladys who looks to Herb. All three look pained and confused. The ENSEMBLE loudly and somewhat desperately repeats a final...)*

ENSEMBLE. Party chatter, party chatter, chatter chatter, party chatter. *(They freeze, then slowly move to their next positions as KIM begins to speak)*

KIM. Pretty rotten, huh? When you're a kid and your

parents lie to you, you never really know what to believe anymore. You never know who to trust, so you trust nobody. One thing I admire about Billy is the way he can hold a grudge. For years after that cocktail party he made their lives miserable. He refused to call them "Mom" or "Dad". They refused to let him call them anything else. So, by the time he was nine, he didn't call them at all. He built a whole new life for himself modelled after the most powerful orphan of all time - Superman! *(In Billy's room. The two chairs belonging to Aunt Margaret and Mr. Lawless are now facing away from center)*

ENSEMBLE. "Faster than a speeding bullet. More powerful than a locomotive. Able to leap tall buildings in a single bound. Look! Up in the sky! It's a bird! It's a plane! It's Superman! *(BILLY enters, putting on glasses; the mild-mannered Clark Kent)*

BILLY. Great Scott! It's that fiendish Lex Luthor. He's planted a bomb in the United Nations Building! Thousands will be killed unless... This looks like a job for... SUPERMAN! *(ENSEMBLE hums a "Superman" theme as he quickly disrobes, revealing a home-made Superman outfit)* Up, up and away! *(He begins to "fly" around the stage, the ENSEMBLE creating the appropriate sound effects. BILLY remains in one position, but the ENSEMBLE moves in the opposite direction, creating the effect of flight. Then, landing...)* Aha! Well, my old friend, Lex Luthor, we meet again. What's that, a laser gun? *(ENSEMBLE creates ray gun sounds: zap. Zap, zap)* Put away your puny weapon. you can't hurt me, I'm invulnerable! Now, let me melt that gun with my heat vision before you hurt yourself. *(ENSEMBLE creates sizzling sound effect. One member begins to make ticking sounds; the rest join in)* Great Krypton! I almost forgot the bomb! *(He flies to the "bomb" and covers it with his body as it exlodes)*

ENSEMBLE. Kapow!!!! *(Herb has quietly entered. He is not pleased)*

HERB. Billy.

BILLY. *(Startled, he turns quickly)* Oh, hi d... Hi.

HERB. What are you doing?

BILLY. Playing.

HERB. Billy, for God's sake, you're almost nine; don't you think you're a little old for... *(Deciding to drop it)* Billy, your mother is very hurt. Is it too much to ask? Is it too much to ask that you call her "Mom"? *(No response)* You treat her, you treat us both like we're strangers. We're your parents, Billy. *(BILLY looks at him defiantly)* We're the only parents you've ever known. *(Trying to be reasonable)* Look, we always meant to tell you, but... One word, Billy. One word, "Mom". Is it too much to ask?

BILLY. Yes.

HERB. What?

BILLY. Yes, it's too much to ask.

HERB. *(Hurt and upset)* Clean up this room, it's a mess. And get rid of that ridiculous costume.

BILLY. *(Picking up his clothes, getting dressed)* Yes, sir. *(HERB begins to leave. He stops, looks back at Billy who freezes)*

HERB. You're a cold one, Billy. Do you know that?

BILLY. Yes, sir. I know that. *(HERB exits, moves to his chair, faces it away from center and sits)* You can't hurt me! I'm invulnerable! *(ENSEMBLE resumes the Superman theme and creates the appropriate sound effects as BILLY "flies" out of the room)*

KIM. I guess I was in the fourth grade when I got to know Billy. We'd been around each other in school since we were little, but we didn't really know each other. He was just this quiet nerdy kid in my class. The only reason I noticed him at all was because, like me, he didn't have any friends. But one day, when we were in the fourth grade we got a chance to get better aquainted at, of all places, the funeral home. *(In the funeral home. The ENSEMBLE, kneeling, murmurs the rosary. BILLY is sitting on the floor reading a Superman comic when KIM enters,*

BILLY. *(Hiding the book)* What are you doing here?

KIM. I'm looking for the girl's room.

BILLY. It's downstairs in the basement.

KIM. *(Crossing to him)* What are you hiding?

BILLY. Nothing.

KIM. If it's nothing, why are you hiding it?

BILLY. If I showed you, you'd probably tell.

KIM. Tell who?

BILLY. My father.

KIM. I don't even know your father.

BILLY. Oh.

KIM. So, what is it?

BILLY. *(Reluctantly)* This.

KIM. Superman?!

BILLY. Yeah.

KIM. *(Kneeling beside him)* He's my favorite.

BILLY. Really?

KIM. Honest.

BILLY. I didn't think girls liked this stuff.

KIM. *I* do. A lot. I used to...

BILLY. What?

KIM. Forget it, you'll think it's dumb.

BILLY. Will not.

KIM. You won't laugh?

BILLY. Promise.

KIM. I used to pretend that Superman was my father.

BILLY. So?

KIM. *(Caught up in her fantasy)* Every night he'd fly in my window. He'd smile, and his eyes would sparkle. Then, he's pick me up in his arms and he'd wrap me in his cape so I wouldn't get cold, and we'd fly up, up and away! *(Remembering that BILLY is there)* Stupid, huh?

BILLY. *(He is moved)* Really stupid.

KIM. Jerk! *(She starts to exit)*

BILLY. Where are you going?

KIM. I gotta get back.

BILLY. Why?

KIM. They'll be looking for me.

BILLY. You better not tell. My father would kill me.

KIM. Why?

BILLY. Well, he runs this place.

KIM. So?

BILLY. You know, funeral director.

KIM. So?

BILLY. You don't think that's funny?

KIM. Why would I?

BILLY. Everybody else does.

KIM. I don't think anyone's father is funny.

BILLY. What's your father do?

KIM. Nothing.

BILLY. Nothing?

KIM. He's dead. That's him in the next room.

BILLY. *(Confused)* Oh, jeez, I'm sorry, I...

KIM. Don't be. I'm not. I'm glad he's dead. *(Exiting)* See ya. *(She exits as the ENSEMBLE prays more loudly, then freezes. They move to their next position as KIM re-enters and speaks)* What can I say? I fell in love with Billy Thompson that day. Partly because of the Superman thing, partly because he was the only kid I knew who seemed as miserable as me, but mostly because I knew that in some way his father had hurt him, like my father hurt me. Hey, don't get all interested and excited. I'm not going to tell you anything about my father 'cause it's none of your business. It's not something I can talk about. It's not even something I let myself think about. All I can say is the day my father died I felt like I was being let out of jail, and Billy Thompson was the first person I met. Of course, Billy pretended that he didn't want anything to do with me, he didn't want anyone to think he needed a friend. But I just kept hanging around the funeral home until he finally let me play Superman. Billy was always Superman. I was either the bad guy who threatened to destroy the earth or, on good days, Krypto the Superdog. Arf! Arf! In private, we were arch enemies, but in school it was different - Billy pretended I didn't exist. *(A classroom. George is in front of the class finishing his report)*

GEORGE. *(Pointing straight up)* ...and that is why the needle of the compass points north! *(Applause from the class as GEORGE takes his seat)*

MRS. TOMMELIO. That was very good work, George, wasn't it, boys and girls?

ENSEMBLE. Yes, Mrs. Tommelio.

MRS. TOMMELIO. Now who would like to next? *(All the kids raise their hands, pleading to be called. KIM tries to hide)* Kim. *(The others giggle as she proceeds to the front of the classroom)*

KIM. *(Unloading a shoe box which contains four rocks painted white, red, green and gold respectively)* My science project is on Kryptonite. Many years ago the planet Kyrpton exploded and pieces of the planet flew through space and some of them landed here on earth. When the pieces left Krypton they were just like rocks or something, but weird things happened to him in space and turned the rocks different colors: white, red, green and gold. Now, if you are an earthling, these rocks won't do anything to you, but if you happen to be from the planet Krypton, it's a different story. The white kryptonite doesn't do that much, it just kills plants and vegetables and stuff like that. The red kryptonite can make you do real strange things, but it doesn't last that long, usually about twenty-four hours, so that's o.k. The green kyrptonite is very dangerous 'cause it can kill you. *(The kids who have been giggling start to look a little nervous)* The gold kryptonite takes away all your super powers forever. *(The kids burst into laughter. Kim becomes angry)* It's not funny! My friend Billy Thompson says the gold is the worst 'cause he wouldn't want to live if he couldn't be invulnerable. *(The kids turn to Billy. He is humiliated)*

BILLY. Did not.
KIM. Did so.
BILLY. Did not.
KIM. You did so.
BILLY. You're not even my friend!

KIM. *(Crushed, turns away from the class)* Stinking liar.

MRS. TOMMELIO. Now, Kim, I...

KIM. *(Screaming)* Crap! *(She runs from the room as the kids freeze. MRS. TOMMELIO moves to her chair, facing it away from center. As KIM re-enters, the ENSEMBLE moves to their next position)* We were in the sixth grade when sex reared its ugly head. In school that morning Mr. Cullen and Mrs. Leonard, the two gym teachers, separated the girls and the boys. The girls were herded into the caf and shown a filmstrip called, "Respect for Your Body." Next, Mrs. Leonard talked about "What It Means to Be A Woman" and "Why Wait Until Marriage?" I had no idea what it was we were supposed to wait to do. The other girls were giggling and giving each other knowing looks. Then it finally hit me. She was talking about sex. So that's what it's all about - never sitting on a boy's lap and learning to say "No". I couldn't wait for the day to end so I could ask Billy what Mr. Cullen said to the boys. *(After school. The two Up Center chairs serve as a doorway. The ENSEMBLE simulates a dismissal bell and then bursts through the door talking, laughing, etc. BILLY rushes in followed by KIM. When he sees her, he bolts, but she chases him around the stage, and perhaps even out into the audience)* Billy. Billy!

BILLY. What?

KIM. Jeez, what's your hurry?

BILLY. I gotta get home.

KIM. Don't you want to...

BILLY. No.

KIM. You don't even know what I was gonna...

BILLY. Stop following me, will you? You're always following me. What are you, my shadow? Can't I even walk down the street...

KIM. Listen, you diseased armpit...

BILLY. Why don't you go play with your dolls or something? Why don't you...

KIM. Dolls? The only doll I ever had was a G.I. Joe and you melted him in the microwave last summer when you were working on your heat vision.

BILLY. *(Looking around nervously as he crosses to her)* Shut up, will you?

KIM. What's the matter, afraid that someone might find out that you're in the sixth grade and *(Screaming)* you still play Superman!

BILLY. I said shut up, pus face!

KIM. Jerk!

BILLY. Snot nose!

KIM. Earwax!

BILLY. Liar!

KIM. *(Stunned)* What?

BILLY. You heard me, you fat, greasy, stupid liar. Always wanting to play tackle, blowing your nose on your sleeve, never taking a bath, looking like something that crawled out of the bottom of a pig pile, and all the time you're a... girl.

KIM. I never said I wasn't, you scab.

BILLY. You just think you're so tough.

KIM. I can take anything you can dish out, creep.

BILLY. Sure...

KIM. Go on, hit me. Hit me as hard as you can, wimp. I can take it. *(Pushing him, then hitting him)* What's the matter? Chicken? Come on, chicken, hit me. Hit me!

BILLY. *(Throwing her down and straddling her)* I don't hit

girls. *(He exits)*

KIM. *(Screaming after him)* Chicken! Slime! Crud! Reject, dipstick, loser, freak! *(Crying in frustration, she spits)* I can still spit farther than you, you sleazy maggot! *(To the audience, as the Ensemble stands on their chairs forming "candles")* You see what a jerk he is? I decided never to talk to that pizza-faced piece of week-old toe jam again. *(Pause)* That lasted about two days. The next time I saw Billy, he pretended that nothing had happened. But something *had* happened. He wouldn't come near me, and if he bumped into me by mistake, he'd get all angry and bent out of shape. And then there was his thirteenth birthday party. He invited everyone in school - except me. *(BILLY'S Birthday Party. The ENSEMBLE quietly sings the words, "Happy Birthday" to the tune of "The Volga Boatmen." BILLY peers out of the window and nervously checks the time. He rearranges the furniture, checks the window again, and begins to fantasize about the party)*

BILLY. Gee, Hank, it sure was nice for all you guys from the football team to come to my party.

BILLY as HANK. No problem, dude. Naturally we wouldn't want to miss a party for a great guy like you.

BILLY. And thanks for all the football stuff, but as you know, I don't play.

BILLY as HANK. But you will. Me and the guys got together and talked to coach. We told him you were a natural athlete. He wants you suited up for the big game.

BILLY. Really! Wow! This is the best birthday... *(Back to reality. A little embarrassed, he moves to the window again. Seeing someone, he quickly checks the room and sits, trying to look cool.*

KIM approaches the door and rings the bill which is sounded by the ENSEMBLE. BILLY crosses to the door and opens it. He is severely disappointed) What are you doing here?

KIM. I'm here for the party.

BILLY. You weren't invited.

KIM. I came anyhow.

BILLY. I don't want you here.

KIM. Tough, I'm staying. *(Crossing into the room)* Hey, this looks great.

BILLY. My mother. I told her not to.

KIM. Why?

BILLY. Crepe paper and party hats? It's embarrassing. I mean I'm practically in high school.

KIM. So?

BILLY. Forget it. You wouldn't understand. *(He crosses to the window)*

KIM. Maybe they got lost.

BILLY. Right.

KIM. The traffic's terrible tonight. They...

BILLY. Hey, don't confuse me with someone who gives a damn. *(Long uncomfortable pause)* You want something to eat?

KIM. Why don't we wait?

BILLY. For what?

KIM. For the others.

BILLY. We might starve. *(KIM thinks that he is making a joke and laughs. BILLY gives her a withering look)*

KIM. I brought you a present.

BILLY. You didn't have to.

KIM. *(Handing him the present)* I wanted to.

BILLY. Thanks.

KIM. Aren't you going to open it? *(He opens the package. He tries to conceal his delight at the gift, a vintage Superman comic. When he says nothing, KIM gets nervous and starts to babble)* I hope you don't already have it. It's my favorite issue. It's real old, that's why the pages are all yellow and stuff. It's a great story. It's... you see, Superman realizes that he loves Lois Lane and he doesn't want to be alone anymore, but he knows that it's impossible, he can't be Superman and be in love - it would be too dangerous, for Lois, you know. So, he decides to give it all up, all of it, and just be Clark Kent. So he flies home to his Fortress of Solitude, and when he gets there he goes right to the lead-lined box where he keeps this piece of gold kryptonite. At first, you don't think he's gonna do it. There's tears in his eyes, I mean, my God, Superman's practically crying, but when he opens the box his face is all gold and warm, and he's smiling. Can you imagine? He's thrown it all away: the flying, the heat vision, invulnerability, everything, and he's smiling now 'cause he hasn't lost his super powers, he's traded them for something more... something more real.

BILLY. Real? It says right here that this is an imaginary issue. It never really happened to Superman.

KIM. I don't care what it says. Maybe it hasn't happened yet, but it will. I mean, who wants to be alone forever?

BILLY. Me.

KIM. Liar!

ENSEMBLE. *(Shouting)* "Happy Birthday, Billy!" *(The ENSEMBLE jumps off their chairs, turns them away from center. All freeze. They move to their next positions as KIM speaks to the audience)*

KIM. I should have cracked him right across his empty head. Needless to say, no one else showed up for the party. It was pathetic. Billy blamed it on his parents and on the fact that they lived in the funeral home. *(Dinner at the Funeral Home. The Thompsons eat dinner. HERB and GLADYS sit at opposite ends of a long "table." BILLY is in the center. The ENSEMBLE, now a collection of corpses, is arranged around the playing area, hands crossed on chests, staring sightlessly out)*

HERB. Did you get a chance to see Mrs. Harrison?

GLADYS. She looked lovely, Herbert.

HERB. Family thought we'd have to have a closed casket.

GLADYS. A beautiful piece of work.

HERB. Frankly, I never thought we'd get her looking so much like herself. Not after what she went through. *(BILLY is totally grossed out by this discussion)*

GLADYS. I recognized her right away.

HERB. There's no substitute for craftsmanship. Remember that, William.

BILLY. Do we have to talk about this at dinner?

GLADYS. Billy, please...

HERB. Watch yourself, William.

BILLY. Isn't it enough that we have to be surrounded by them?

GLADYS. Billy, I think you'd better...

BILLY. Isn't it enough that we have to live with them, that it's like some grade B horror movie around here with corpses in every room? Do we have to talk about them at dinner, too? It's disgusting.

HERB. *(Rising and crossing to BILLY)* Disgusting is it?

Well isn't that just too damn bad. Like it or not dead people are my business, and it's a damn good business. Dead people put clothes on your back. Dead people paid for your dental work. Dead people put food on this table and a roof over your head, and if you don't like it, you can just...

GLADYS. Herbert!

BILLY. Leave? *(He rushes out. HERB and GLADYS try to resume eating, but, disgusted, HERB throws down his napkin, returns his chair to a position facing away from center and stares at GLADYS as she returns her chair facing in. They exchange challenging glances. Finally, GLADYS turns her chair facing away from center and sits. HERB then sits. The ENSEMBLE becomes various young campers perparing for bed as KIM enters)*

KIM. During the summer after our sophomore year, I sent Billy a letter from camp. *(She settles the campers for the night, then shuts off the lights)* Goodnight, muskrats!

ENSEMBLE. Goodnight, Kim! *(BILLY enters with a letter and begins to read)*

KIM. Dear Billy, This seems so weird. I mean, we've known each other since the fourth grade but this is the first time I've ever had to write to you. Unless you count the time I spray-painted that obscenity on your locker last fall, the day after you told me you put worms in my tuna salad sandwich and made me throw up in the caf in front of the entire sophomore class and Mr. Bolecknee who never liked me in the first place 'cause I fell asleep in his biology class two days in a row. *(Thinking)* Is that a run-on sentence? I would've paid more attention in English class if I ever realized that I might actually have to use that stuff some day. *(She pauses to look around)* This camp

sucks eggs. I'm what they call a C.I.T. which means
Counsellor in Training which means that they work us
like slaves and they don't have to pay us. I spend the
whole day running around after the most pathetic group
of bed-wetting, nail-biting, runny-nosed eight-year-olds
the world has ever seen. And this place is a wilderness.
Everywhere you look trees, trees, and more trees. It
could make you crazy. What I wouldn't give for one piece
of white kryptonite. I'd destroy every piece of vegetation
within a hundred miles of this hell-hole. *(Working herself
into a huff)* I hate this place. I hate my mother for making
me come here. I hate myself for letting her make me
come here. But most of all I hate you for not even coming
to say goodbye before I left. I got your number, Billy,
don't think I don't. You avoided me 'cause you were
pissed that I let myself be talked into coming here and
because you thought that if you came to say goodbye I
might get all emotional and, God forbid, embarrass you,
and maybe you even realized that you were gonna miss
me and maybe *you'd* get all emotional though what a
laugh that is - you emotional, ha, ha, and I don't care if
this is a run-on sentence 'cause you make me sick, you
weaselly scumbag and I don't miss you one stinking bit!
*(She pauses, almost out of breath. One of the campers, in the throes
of a nightmare, moans. KIM goes to comfort her. The ENSEMBLE
simulates forest noises. KIM shivers, then remembering the letter,
continues)* It's scary here when it gets dark. There's all
these weird sounds in the woods, and the campers get
homesick and have nightmares and I spend half the night
trying to calm them down. I tell them stories. Superman
stories. I know it's dumb but those are the only stories I

know and besides the kids love them. When they get real scared I tell them to wrap their blankets around them in a certain way, and it's like Superman's cape - it will keep them safe. And they believe me. They ask me stuff. Yesterday, Donna Sue Hadden asked me if I had a boyfriend. I said I didn't know. *(She takes a deep breath)* Well, I better stop here so I won't have to start a new paragraph. I always stunk at paragraphs. Your..........? Kim. P.S. You better write to me soon! *(BILLY stands, puts the letter in his pocket. KIM anxiously takes an envelope from her pocket and rips it open)*

BILLY. Dear Kim, I got your letter. Billy. *(Kim, furious, rips his letter to shreds. As she speaks, the ENSEMBLE moves to their next positions)*

KIM. Can you believe him? Can you? When I got home at the end of the summer I refused to call him. And of course, there was no way that he was gonna call me first. But I didn't care. I didn't. I wasn't going to let him drag me down. When school started that Fall, I joined the drama club. It was great! It was the one place in that whole stinking school where it was o.k. to be weird. I loved to act; pretending to be someone else was such a relief. And if I missed Billy, I never let it show. I'd see him around school and give him a big, "Hey, how's it going?" and hurry away before he could answer. 'Cause it was obvious that things were going pretty bad for him. He looked like one of those guys from NIGHT OF THE LIVING DEAD, all blank-faced and scary. *His* mother called *my* mother. She was desperate. She wanted to talk to me but I refused. I wasn't gonna get sucked in. Herb and Gladys must have been in a total panic by the time they forced Billy to see a psychiatrist. *(The psychiatrist's office. All chairs are facing in. The ENSEMBLE assumes the role of DR. ANGLE, speaking and moving as one person. BILLY enters)*

BILLY. I just want you to know right from the beginning that I don't want to be here.

DR. ANGLE. I see.

BILLY. It's just a waste of money. I told my father that he could make me come here, but he couldn't make me talk.

DR. ANGLE. Mm hmm.

BILLY. I don't care what they think, I'm not crazy.

DR. ANGLE. No?

BILLY. No. And I'm sick of it. Either they treat me like dirt or they tip-toe around me like I'm some kinda lunatic. Why can't they just leave me alone?

DR. ANGLE. Alone.

BILLY. Damn straight. I don't need their concern, and I don't want it. Maybe I do have problems, but nothing I can't handle.

DR. ANGLE. Really.

BILLY. It's this whole adoption thing. My parents are so paranoid about it. I mean, big deal, right? Lots of people are adopted. I just saw this thing in the paper about this family in Florida. They adopted this kid, and he turned out to be a real loser, a juvenile delinquent type, you know, drugs, stealing. So after fifteen years of living with the kid they try to *un*adopt him. I mean, what's that got to do with me? I don't give them any trouble.

DR. ANGLE. Is that so.

BILLY. They just think I'm strange. They think I don't have any friends. Shows you how much they know, I have millions of friends. My mother's always saying, "Then why don't you ask one of them home to dinner?" I mean, really, who wants to eat dinner in a funeral home? I mean, it doesn't bother me, I'm used to it, but it would ruin most people's appetites.

DR. ANGLE. I see.

BILLY. And there's this girl. God, she's been following me around for years, and then, all of a sudden, it's like I'm radioactive. She won't come near me. But I don't care, I don't want her to like me. It's the people who supposedly like you who can do the most damage. I don't want anything from anybody. I just want to be left alone, is that too much to ask?

DR. ANGLE. Yes.

BILLY. What?

DR. ANGLE. Yes, it's too much to ask. *(BILLY looks stunned. One by one the members of the ENSEMBLE turn their chairs away from center, then freeze. They move to their next position as KIM begins to speak)*

KIM. It really pissed me off, they were all ganging up on him. Why can't a kid be different without sixteen adults jumping on his back trying to make him a happy, carefree adolescent? There are a million reasons to be angry, confused, scared and unhappy, but the minute you stop smiling, they ship you off to a shrink. It was clear that Billy needed my help, but I didn't want to fall back into our old relationship. I wanted romance, sex, anything to show me that I wasn't alone, that we did have something between us, that it wasn't just Superman and Krypto. That it was us, Kim and Billy, Billy and Kim. I thought, maybe all boys were stupid. It's not like I had tons of experience. Maybe he just needs a little push. *(Starting to plan)* So, I decided to put my newly acquired drama training to use and stage a little scene. First, I called him up. *(She dials. The ENSEMBLE makes the appropriate sound effects: touch tone sounds, phone ringing)* Billy, this is Kim. I'll meet you at my house at 8:30. *(ENSEMBLE: Click!)* When he called back *(ENSEMBLE: Ringing telephone)* I didn't answer. I knew he'd show up out of curiosity if nothing else. Next, I checked the setting - my living room. *(ENSEMBLE rearranges the furniture)* Then, some romantic music in the background. *(She snaps her fingers and the ENSEMBLE starts to hum a drippy love song)* And finally, but most importantly, the lighting. *(She snaps her fingers and the stage goes black)* Perfect. *(BILLY has entered during the blackout)* Well, here we are.

BILLY. Yeah. It sure is...

KIM. What?

BILLY. Dark.

KIM. Oh.

BILLY. Very dark.

KIM. I thought it would be better.

BILLY. Than what? Light?

KIM. Well...

BILLY. It's not bad.

KIM. No...

BILLY. Once you get used to it.

KIM. Good. *(Pause)* Well...

BILLY. Yeah?

KIM. Why don't you move closer.

BILLY. Why?

KIM. Because.

BILLY. Why because?

KIM. Unbelievable.

BILLY. What?

KIM. You are unbelievable. Don't you know anything? Don't you even know what you're supposed to do? Can't you... take some initiative? *(A noise)* Ow! What was that?

BILLY. That was me trying to take some initiative.

KIM. That's a relief. I thought you were trying to beat me to death with your forehead. *(A movement)* Hey, where do you think you're going? Billy?

BILLY. *(Turns on lights. Stage is flooded with light)* Is that supposed to be funny? Is it? Is that supposed to be funny?

KIM. Oh, for...

BILLY. *(Beginning to lose control)* I am sick and tired of you, always mocking me, always with the mouth. One minute you're all lovey-dovey: "Billy, be my boyfriend, Billy kiss me, Billy hold me. Billy love me," but the minute I trust you, you take out the knife and cut me to pieces. Well, forget it, just forget it. You've busted on me for the last time. I don't need this. I don't need you. From now on just keep away from me...

KIM. *(Upset, crossing to him)* Billy, I...

BILLY. *(Recoiling as she reaches to him)* Leave me alone! *(He rushes from the room. The ENSEMBLE continues the romantic music until KIM furiously "snaps" them off)*

KIM. All right, all right, I admit it. I blew it. It was stupid. The whole stupid relationship was stupid. Dumb, dumb, dumb. I was ready to chuck the whole thing, I didn't need the aggravation. And, of course, things got worse between us. Every time we'd get together we'd fight, but whenever we weren't together we'd be miserable. So, I got more involved with drama, and Billy started hanging with a group of jerks at school. It was awful. They just kept him around for comic relief, but Billy refused to see it. Until Halloween night. That was the night Billy stole a bottle of his father's scotch, and his father's hearse. *(Halloween Night. BILLY and KIM are in the hearse. BILLY is driving. He is wearing his Superman costume)*

KIM. This is stupid. This is the stupidest thing you've ever done.

BILLY. Shut up, will you?

KIM. When your father finds out you stole this hearse, he's going to kill you.

BILLY. *(Drinking scotch from the bottle and gagging)* I'm terrified.

KIM. You're going to get sick!

BILLY. Jeez.

KIM. You are.

BILLY. You're going to make me sick.

KIM. Billy, you don't even know these kids. Two weeks ago they wouldn't even say "hi" to you and now they're all buddy-buddy 'cause you got something they want.

BILLY. You don't know what...

KIM. They're using you. They are, they're...

BILLY. *(Pulling over)* Get out.

KIM. What?

BILLY. You're not going to ruin this. Get out.

KIM. *(Getting out of the hearse)* Do you think I care? Do you? Well I don't. *(She slams the door closed as BILLY pulls away from the curb)* Go ahead, have a great time with your friends, but don't you ever talk to me again. I hate you. *(Screaming)* I hate you, Billy! *(BILLY continues to drink from the bottle as he drives. Finally he pulls over and stops the hearse)*

MARTY. Hey, all right, he got it! *(The other kids enter)*

DAVE. *(As BILLY gets out of the hearse)* Good work, Superman. *(The other kids laugh)*

BILLY. *(To Marty)* You said everyone was going to wear costumes.

MARTY. Did I?

BILLY. Yeah, you said...

MARTY. Well, I guess we changed our minds. *(The other kids find this hysterical)*

BILLY. Jeez...

MARTY. *(To Dave)* Where's the beer?

DAVE. Come on, Billy-boy, lighten up. This is going to be a Halloween to remember. Let's get this show on the road! *(They form the back of the hearse with their chairs, then crawl in)*

MARTY. This is gonna be fantastic! Come on, everybody in. First stop, the cemetery! *(Lots of noise and laughter from the kids. BILLY sulks at a distance)*

DAVE. Let's fly, Superman! *(BILLY closes the rear door, gets in the driver's seat and starts the hearse)*

MARTY. *(Handing him a beer)* There you go, big guy. Crank up some music, will you?

BILLY. There's no radio.

MARTY. Aw, man.

SUE. *(Shrieking)* Dave, stop it!

DAVE. It was an accident, I thought that was *my* leg.

(Howls of laughter from the kids)

MARTY. Let's make our own music. *(He begins the song, the others join in. He keeps prodding them to sing faster)*

ENSEMBLE. "Did you ever think when a hearse goes by that you might be the next to die? They wrap you up in a big white sheet and bury you about six feet deep. All goes well for about a week and then the casket begins to leak. The worms crawl in, the worms crawl out, the worms play pinochle on your snout. You toss and turn until you're green and puss comes out like fresh whipped cream."

MARTY. Faster, faster. *(They continue to sing at an increased speed. Every time MARTY yells "faster" BILLY depresses the gas pedal a little more. Suddenly, one of the girls screams. Startled, BILLY turns to them)*

BILLY. Hey, take it easy, will you? *(When he turns back to the road, he sees that he has wandered out of his lane. Shocked, he tries to overcompensate by yanking the wheel in the other direction. The hearse spins out of control. The kids in the back scream. Blackout. The ENSEMBLE creates the sounds of various sirens, etc. As the lights fade up, KIM enters. The ENSEMBLE is back in their chairs simulating the p.a. system at a hospital, improvising announcements. BILLY, in a bathrobe, is sitting in a chair removed from the others)*

KIM. When I heard about the accident, I barfed my dinner all over the living room carpet. I was so pissed off. At Billy, at myself, at all those jerky kids. Of course no one got hurt, except Billy. He was in the hospital and wouldn't let anyone visit him. But I was sick of getting shut out. *(In the hospital. All the chairs are facing away from center. The hospital noises get louder as KIM opens the door to BILLY'S room, and softer as she closes the door behind her. At first,*

BILLY does not see her) Hi.

BILLY. *(Startled)* How'd you get in? I told them...

KIM. I snuck in.

BILLY. Well, sneak out. *(She doesn't move)* Nurse! *(No response. He reaches for the call button, but this causes him pain)* Aw...

KIM. Does it hurt?

BILLY. Please go.

KIM. Why? *(No response)* Why, Billy?

BILLY. I don't want you to see me like this.

KIM. Like what? *(BILLY can't explain. He indicates his general condition)* Vulnerable? Billy, it's no good pretending. It doesn't work. It's no good pretending that nothing can hurt you. I ought to know. When my father died, I swore I'd never let anyone hurt me again, I'd never let anyone close enough. I'd be tough and I'd be strong, and I'd... I'd build my own Fortress of Solitude where no one could reach me, where no one could hurt me, where I'd be safe. And I am tough, Billy. I am. and I'm strong. But I don't want to be safe anymore if it means I have to be alone.

BILLY. I don't know what you're talking about.

KIM. You do. You do know.

BILLY. Please, I...

KIM. I brought you a present. *(She crosses and places it on his lap)*

BILLY. You didn't have to.

KIM. I wanted to. *(For a moment, they are at ease remembering an earlier occasion. But BILLY fights it)*

BILLY. I don't want it.

KIM. Tough.

BILLY. Leave me alone.

KIM. Not until you open your present. *(BILLY, momentarily resigned, tries to open the box, but is having a difficult time of it because of his injuries. KIM starts to help him, but he glares at her and she retreats. He finally gets the box open, sees what's inside. He is visibly moved)*

BILLY. *(Somewhere between laughter and tears)* Gold Kryptonite?

KIM. I love you, Billy.

BILLY. *(Trying not to cry)* No...

KIM. Yes. I love you.

BILLY. Please...

KIM. *(Defiant, almost angry)* I love you, Billy Thompson, and there's not a damn thing you can do about it. *(She starts to leave)*

BILLY. Kim? *(She stops, turns. He raises the piece of Kryptonite)* Help me?

KIM. *(For a moment, she is stunned. Then with a big smile)* Why not? *(To the audience)* Well, what do you know. Progress. Now, don't get all excited, this doesn't necessarily mean happy ending. It's just the end of a slow beginning. I still think love stinks and I'd rather have terminal acne than be in love. Because the minute you actually say "I love you," you've risked everything, nothing will ever be the same. And you've opened yourself up to the possibility of a whole truck-load of pain. *(Smiling now)* But, no pain, no gain, right? And, for better or worse, I do love Billy Thompson. And he loves me. At least, he better. So, maybe there's the possibility for a whole truck-load of happiness, too. I figure we got about a 50/50 chance. I can live with those odds. *(KIM crosses to Billy. The ENSEMBLE begins to hum the "Superman" theme as the lights fade.)*

CURTAIN

MURDER AT THE GREY'S HOUND MANSION
Maxine Holmgren

Mystery, High School/ Community Theatre / 5f, 3m/ Simple Set
This is a mysterious comedy (or a comical mystery) that will have everyone howling with laughter.

The eccentric owner of Grey's Hound Mansion has been murdered. The cast gathers at the gloomy mansion for the reading of the will. Lightning lights up the stage as thunder and barking dogs greet the wacky characters that arrive. Each one is a suspect, and each one suspects another. Mixed metaphors and alliterations will have the audience barking up the wrong tree until the mystery is solved.

Baker's Plays
7611 Sunset Blvd.
Los Angeles, CA 90046
Phone: 323-876-0579
Fax: 323-876-5482

BAKERSPLAYS.COM

Breinigsville, PA USA
07 December 2010
250625BV00010B/3/P